THE HERMITAGE

THE HERMITAGE

MARIE BRONSARD

Translated from the French
by Sonia Alland

with Marie Bronsard

hydra
books

Northwestern University Press
Evanston, Illinois

Hydra Books
Northwestern University Press
Evanston, Illinois 60208-4210

Originally published in French under the title *L'Ermitage* in 1986.
Copyright © 1986 by Le temps qu'il fait. English translation copyright
© 2001 by Hydra Books/Northwestern University Press. Published
2001. All rights reserved.

Printed in the United States of America
10 9 8 7 6 5 4 3 2 1

ISBN 0-8101-1848-3

Library of Congress Cataloging-in-Publication Data

Bronsard, Marie.
  [Ermitage. English]
  The hermitage / Marie Bronsard ; translated from the French by
Sonia Alland with Marie Bronsard.
    p. cm.
  "Hydra Books."
  ISBN 0-8101-1848-3
  I. Alland, Sonia. II. Title.
  PQ2662.R5827 E7613 2001
  843'.914—dc21

                                                    00-012905

For B.A.

THE HERMITAGE

I began writing to you a long time ago now. Time passed. I kept writing to you. I stopped because I was growing old.

One day a friend of yours I met by chance mentioned your name. I smiled, vague.

When I got home, I burned all that correspondence you never received. It was yesterday.

Today I begin again. There is no hope and I know it. No hope at all of seeing you again, ever. No hope at all of reaching you.

It is a beautiful day, cold but crystal clear, just the kind of day that follows a full moon.

One feels the coming of autumn.

Winter, that was your season.

I remember, the winter you left, you told me: I hate summer. I didn't understand.

It seems to me sometimes that I understand you a little better.

I often find myself, still, walking in the street returning from somewhere. I even find myself thinking of you on the way, you who used to say that night is not made for sleeping. You used to say that one should live, at night, that it alone offers us enough concentration to feel alive.

You see, I have forgotten nothing. I remember everything: your words, your tone of voice, the soft light you gave to each remark, that calmed like the caress of a child.

I remember everything. You cannot remember me.

Such a long time ago. We were young. We had lived very little.

I am almost ten years older.

After you left . . .

After you left, I often thought I saw you coming down a street, sitting on the terrace of a café, a silhouette, a gesture, that strange sway of the shoulders, out of step, that you had when you walked. It could not be you.

Each time, a jolt in my chest, the heart tightening up, it seems, just before it collapses. It was never you.

A long time after, even now, I find myself imagining I recognize you. Never here anymore, though—elsewhere, always elsewhere, as if elsewhere it were easier for me to find you.

I am less and less disappointed. I understand better and better the meaning of your absence.

One day, I will stop believing I recognize you among those who pass by. One day.

One day, I will stop writing to you.

Not today. Tomorrow, perhaps. I fear that, for me, it will be a defeat.

You, you will never come to find me again. You have forgotten me as stones forget, in silence.

Forget . . . to forget you, what long I prayed for with all my body, with all my sadness, with all my lost sleep, forgetfulness which came, little by little, to replace memory without ever erasing it completely.

I will never forget you.

For some time I've no longer been certain that I loved you. Now and then I feel I didn't. Yet I know that I must have loved you but that I'd stopped well before you left. You knew that. You knew, without suffering. You never loved me.

We didn't love each other. We were alone, in that frightening solitude of children who have grown up too fast, who have lost their mooring somewhere in adolescence and who will never find it again. If we loved each other . . . if we'd been able to love each other, it would have been only because of this very solitude.

You remember, the concern we had for one another all during those late nights, that care, precise, exacting, not to tear at each other, not to let others tear at the two of us. At least not until . . . but I don't want to think about it.

I remember those words we exchanged in the night that united us much better than the love we made so badly.

You don't remember. I alone remember.
It seems to me sometimes that my life will not be long enough to take in both of us.

Evening is beginning to fall. Mist will rise from the garden in just a while. The air will turn cold. I'll be cold again. You knew how sensitive I was to the cold. You used to smile about it as if it were a strange caprice. You didn't want to believe that one's body could feel the cold when the soul is frozen.

You, you were never cold, never hungry either, never sleepy. You would drop off to sleep at dawn, like a kitten in the middle of a game, on a chair, among cushions on the floor, in a corner of the room. Never in bed. One had to wake you to lead you to it. You would have a hunted look then, hostile, that made me tremble.

I used to leave you when you were lying there. I'd return to my isolation.

I would so like to talk to you about something other than all this past. For example, how it happens that every evening, as I return home, a black cat crosses my path on the road. It's never the same one, never in the same place, but every evening.

For several years, I've given up going to the city. Without you, it paid no attention to me.

After you left . . . but there I go, talking about it again. Everything, this evening, takes me back to you.

After you left, I still walked alone in the streets, at night, often. I would stop in our cafés. I'd wait for you, sitting at the edge of a dirty table. I used to think I was waiting for you. We so loved those late-night cafés, shabby, sticky, suspicious, always open. People recognized me. They didn't talk to me, not any more than before. I could have thought that nothing had changed, I felt the same. Yet when their silence altered, imperceptibly, turning thicker, heavier as I entered, any faith in that thought was denied me.

It was as if they had guessed, all those others, that you had left intending never to return, as if they knew that from then on I was going to remain alone. They didn't pity me. They kept silent.

In those cafés, the same, always, where I would drink cheap brandy that burned my throat, where I would smoke cigarettes until weary, until closing, I waited for you a very long time.

The café just below where you lived closed the following summer. It did not reopen.

In June, one morning, the first morning in June, I returned there for the last time. The floor was thick with sawdust. I didn't recognize the place.

It was in that café we had met him. That café is closed.

I would like it never to open again.

To continue.

For a long time, I wandered into our sordid cafés, staying until night's end. I thought I was waiting for you.

One day, I grew tired of waiting for you like that. I began once again to walk in the streets, in other neighborhoods, those we had never frequented, those you claimed not to like. I sought out other places. I tried. They remained as foreign to me as ever. Often I was made to leave. No one recognized me. You were no longer there to protect me. You were no longer there to justify my presence.

I stopped.

Then I stopped walking in the streets. I stopped going out.

All that was a long time after you left, when I understood you would never come back again. That pain, that silence, in me. . . .

This night will not be a night like the others. I will write to you, if necessary, until morning. I will write to you until my memories are worn away, until this pain that I begin to feel from remembering is worn away.

I had stopped loving you by the time you left. Before, I no longer remember very well. It seems to me that I desired you the first time and that afterward it was too late. We were already too much in need of one another. You told me that one night: We found each other. We will never understand each other. We have nothing to share. We offer each other nothing, only time, which is nothing. We will never be able to part.

Yet, it was you who left.

You had . . . you were rough in your tenderness, but in the worst moments, in the midst of your harshest words, you had that gentle tilt of the head, that delicate tone of voice which immediately assuaged the suffering you had provoked. Each time, you subjugated me.

You demonstrated such gentleness only when you had placed me, placed us, once again in the middle of the desert, only when you had banned me, banned us, from the oases forever. True despair is just that: no longer being able to cry out.

You were calm, so calm. When I was upset, you would stop me with a smile. You used to say: What good will it do? I would stop.

You were never violent, rarely sad, each day the same as the day before, just as cold. Only your look, the intensity of your silence, betrayed you.

I used to leave you at daybreak, after the dreadful way you'd glance at me which frightened me so. Evening would bring me back. I have no memory at all of the daytime. During the day, I must have slept. Still, it seems that I didn't, that I didn't always sleep. I don't know anymore. Perhaps I would work. Perhaps I would sleep. Perhaps both. I don't remember.
I so well remember you.

In the evening, I'd return to your place. Sometimes you were still sleeping. I would lie down, without a sound, next to you. I would close my eyes. I knew your look, I refused it.
You used to wake up slowly. We'd make love, like people drowning.

Often you were no longer asleep. It was painful for me to approach you. You would remain lying as if dead near the window, prostrated by a terrifying, pent-up anxiety, so powerful that one was ready to believe the walls were going to collapse at any moment. One was not allowed to speak. Not allowed to say a word to you. One had to wait, to wait in silence, sitting, never standing, you couldn't bear it. Wait, sitting, until you could speak again.

After a while, you would say a few words. A murmur.

Never again, after we met him, did I find you asleep.

I am here, at my table, in front of the window. The night is cool. It is falling, pale, misty, artificial. The cars on the hill across the way glide along. I like the slowed-up movement of their lights sweeping the road at the turns. Few houses are lit. On my right, the night seems whiter.

I have learned since you left to love the country-side.

I've not been able to give up totally the feeling of a street, to allow you to part from me altogether. I live in a compromise, on the edge of a village.

I will never be an other.

I would like to talk with you, keep talking with you, hold you back, prevent you from leaving once again. For me, this evening, you are here. I know that in the morning you will leave. Ten years later, this will be your true departure, the true end to the story.

The past is always a story. One recounts it, one repeats it to others, always to others, often, so often that, finally, one no longer knows. Over the years, over the nights, a detail comes to be added, then another, another. . . . One has recounted so often that the words come out of one's mouth by themselves, they string together, follow one another, escape as the past escapes us. One cannot be sure of anything, not even of the past.

Ten years for you, for me. Ten years for me, alone. You will never know.

The morning you left—you went away one morning—you refused to sleep. You tried to drive me out at daybreak. I wanted to stay. It seems to me that I thought for a moment you were waiting for him and that I said as much. It seems to me that you shuddered, that you looked at me in a strange manner. It seems to me that I was so frightened that I stretched my hand toward the door to go out. It seems to me that you held me back by the shoulder, that you touched me, and that then you announced: I'm going to leave. I don't know when I'll be back. I'll write you. Then it seems to me that you pushed me, very gently, outside. It seems to me. I can't be sure of anything anymore all of a sudden. Everything is jumbled up. I have a headache.

You had perhaps warned me during the night. Perhaps I knew for a long time that you were going to leave. Perhaps. No. I didn't know. I couldn't know. For a long time you had not said anything. I didn't know. You didn't know either. Not the night before any more than the preceding days. We'd spent a night similar to many others. He had not come. We had not left the room. We were no longer waiting for him.

That morning, you said to me: I'm going to leave. That morning. I was not surprised. I went out. I began to wait for you. We had never been separated, never written to each other. You were always there, every night, me too. Even when you were with him, I was with you. You never wanted me to stay away. During the day, only the day, when you were sleeping, was I to be somewhere else.

Soon, ten years since you left. Ten years that I know you will no longer be coming back.

I would like the mildness of the night to cease. I would like it to rain. It's not going to rain. The sky is too clear.
You will not be coming back. You never wrote to me.

I began to wait for you from the moment you announced you were leaving. I was there, near you, standing just in front of the door, but already I was waiting for you. I could see you. I could touch you. But already I felt you were gone. I asked nothing. Nothing. It would have been useless. I didn't question myself about your return. I began to wait for you. I went out. You closed the door after me with a gentle gesture, which I have perhaps invented since.

Did you know it? I don't think so. What did you know about this departure? You said: I'll write you. Then nothing. A long silence. Ten years. You will not be coming back again.

The wind has picked up. I hear the trees, the leaves of the trees. The house is silent. Night is here now altogether, a milky night, a night of the full moon. People say one should fear these nights. I am alone. I am not afraid.

I was never again frightened of the night, of the silence, after I met you. Your departure has changed nothing. You brought me serenity, emptiness. I'm never anxious anymore. I wait for the moment to pass, for day to return. I wait without impatience. Nothing more can happen to me.

The next day, the day after that, I no longer remember, they came to tell me. I didn't understand. I continued to wait for you.

I know. One day this waiting must end. As even

the memory of you must. The ability is there, within me. I know. Now and then I forget. I have to acknowledge it. I long for forgetfulness. It frightens me. I would so like to keep you within me, intact but not part of me.

I couldn't keep anything of you. I had nothing. All that remained was in your room, on the walls of your room, those ugly green and white walls that we'd covered together with words, with phrases. You did not like those walls but you didn't make the slightest change. You sometimes drew broad curves on them that you used to call your circles of destiny. They terrified me. You'd say they were necessary, the necessary witnesses to the absence of life. I didn't like them, no more than I did the walls which, alone, have preserved the mark left by your passage.

The walls and my memory.

A night bird cried in the forest behind the house, a cry of pain that died away slowly. It seems to me at present that the silence is thicker, that nothing can tear it apart again until forgetfulness comes, of this cry. I would like never to forget it. I would like it to fix beside you in my memory, a long sigh in a beautiful night, to serve as your breath, as your life. Now I can no longer remember you without this cry. I'm glad to have finally drawn you out of your silence. This bird, his call in the night, is perhaps a little of you. Perhaps. One cannot know. I will never know anything more about you.

I knew nothing about you. You never spoke of the past. Neither did I. What would we have had to say, life had not started? In front of him only, you occasionally evoked moments from your childhood, for him, and I hated him because of it.

I so hated him. I hated him the very instant you looked at him, the first time, in the café.

He was at the bar. He stood with his back to us. One could see his face in the mirror, among the bottles. His eyes were closed. You looked at him. I hated him. You had never looked that way at anyone, at anything. I still hate him. My hatred persists, absolute, undiminished, in spite of the years. Hatred, alone, has lasted. Only a shadow remains of the steady pain that was your departure. This hatred of him still pierces my stomach.

I would so have liked not to talk about him, not to think about it. There he is, asserting himself again. There he is, moving you farther off. He keeps his power over you even in my memory.

His closed eyes. . . . Perhaps it was those eyes that attracted you, like a look, doubled, like a troubled look, like trouble. . . .

I wanted to go away. I wanted us to leave. I remember I said: We mustn't stay. I feel danger in the air. You answered: It's already too late. Anything can happen.
You took my hand. You squeezed it very hard, too hard. You led us over to him, to the bar.

I didn't see him after you left. I knew he was in the city. I wasn't afraid of meeting him. I didn't seek him out.
If I had crossed his path, I would have killed him.

When you left, it was winter, a cold winter day, leaden. It was going to snow. One hoped it would. Everything felt too heavy. There was a kind of tension in the gray air. I walked in the lights of the passing cars.
I crossed the city. I walked a long time. Evening

came, bringing the snow. I went back, all the way to your room. I knocked.

I knew but I knocked.

I have no memory at all of the night after you went away.

Spring arrived, I walked, then summer, I continued to walk. I had changed neighborhoods. I began to hate summer, like you, without understanding why exactly. I detested the clear light, the sun, the more transparent water of the river. At night, I'd go into the parks to trample the flowers. The street was no longer ours. It was invaded by others. I started hating it as well.

When autumn came, I stopped going out.

The night is clear and calm. The moon has changed its place. I am writing as the night begins. The shadow of the trees is smaller. At this hour, the moon overwhelms. The deep silence of the forest fills the house. I dare not move. The slightest gesture would rip it apart.

Another night, a night of the full moon, we walked in the streets. It seems to me it was winter. For me, with you, it was always winter.

You led me to the edge of the river. It was cold. We sat down, far from each other. We looked at the lights of the city reflecting off the surface of the black water. You spoke to me about him. You spoke to me about his somber eyes and his laugh. He knew how to laugh. He had the habit of bursting suddenly into loud, painful laughter, of stopping short, breaking it off. You, you never used to laugh. His laugh would fascinate you. You admired it for being childlike. You admired him and I hated him for knowing you were capable of speaking about it in such a way.

That evening, he hadn't come. You'd waited for him a bit, then we'd gone out. You were sad. You knew it was useless to keep waiting, that he'd no longer be coming before the next day. You were sad. You talked to me about him. You talked to yourself about him. I kept quiet.

I know that you didn't love him, any more than you loved me. He had become necessary to you, like another self, spontaneous, immediate. His words were biting, his gestures impulsive. He laughed at what caused you to smile. He screamed when you no more than pursed your lips. He flared up with anger when you simply shrugged your shoulders in cold disapproval. He seemed alive to you. It seemed he was offering you life. Him, you never asked: What good will it do?

The evening of the full moon, we remained on the bank for a very long time. You talked about him. I said nothing. I listened. I was frozen. I no longer had the strength to tremble. Several times you got up to leave. You kept saying: A coffee will warm us. I didn't get up. I knew too well that you were going to sit down again. You were too frightened of meeting him without his wanting it.

When he didn't come, it was forbidden to look for him, forbidden to wait for him. He used to say that one cannot meet by chance more than once. He used to say that he would not see you again the day he would no longer be free to choose.

We remained at the river's edge the entire night. When morning came, we returned to your place. You were shivering. Your eyes were shining with fever. We were exhausted. I could no longer even articulate. Yet it seemed to me that you were almost happy for the first time. You had resisted the desire to see him. You were sick from it. You expected recognition for it.

It is perhaps that morning I stopped loving you.

How grand the night is. I would prefer it opaque. It has an end-of-the-world light. I have not closed the shutters. I will not close them. This night belongs to me as I belong to it.

You remember, in the middle of the night, we'd search in the bottom of a glass of brandy. He used to say that there was nothing to search for, nothing to find. He used to laugh and you stopped believing in it.
As for me, I was never certain.

He would say . . . he talked so much. He only talked to you. I was there, he would forget about me.

You would forget about me. I kept quiet. I never addressed a word to him directly.

The first evening, we drew near. I followed you. You were holding my hand. We remained at his side a long time, in silence. We were drinking. He was alone. We hardly counted as two. We stayed on. Closing hour came. I thought . . . I said: Let's go. He looked at us. He seemed to discover we were there. Calmly, he asked: Where are you going? I thought I would die when you answered: Wherever you want. He smiled. He acknowledged you. He led us away.

That first evening, he said nothing more.

How slowly this night passes. One might say that it is hesitating. One might say that it is holding itself back at the edge of dawn, that it refuses to let itself be erased by the day.

It is still too early. Already I grow impatient. There is too much of us, of him, in this night.

After you left, I often played at remembering. I would try to find you again, to hold you in that place where memories converge. I never came upon you.

At the end of some time, a sort of weariness overcame me, a shadow, a weariness . . . that sort of unsettled fatigue which softens the angles of revolt, which completes the banal circle of despair.

My weariness.

Long after you left, I stopped going out. I don't remember the rest. They told me. I don't remember anymore. A hallway. A closed door. A door that I passed through one day. One day, I walked along the hall and opened the door. It was a long time ago, a very long time, a longer time than you have been gone, it seems to me. Someone told me. I don't remember anymore. The effort I would need to remember again would be dreadful. So much energy expended for nothing. The time is without any importance.

As soon as I think of you, I think of him. As soon as I think of him, memories crystallize. I remember everything, the hour, the quality of his voice, of yours, your words, the depth of my silence. I remember everything, the walks across the city at night, the hesitations that took hold of us at dawn when the moment came to part.

He would go off before I did. He left us alone with a last ironic look, scornful, to which we could not respond. I cannot say what he knew about us. He must have sensed in an obscure way that nothing happened, while he was gone, but your sleep. No doubt he wanted to prevent the reawakening of something he could not, in all decency, forbid. He extinguished in us the very idea of desire.

Ten years later, tonight, here he is threatening us once again.

I would so like to remember the evening we came upon each other for the first time, but memories are fading. All that's left is a sensation of evening's approach, of twilight. It is engraved deep within my body, half hidden by the memory of the first night.

Where, how, did I first meet you? Who introduced us? I think I remember there was never anyone else between us, never anyone but him.

One evening, somewhere, we found each other. One evening, followed by a night. That first night, I remember.

The first night, you took me to your room. We sat on the floor, side by side. We talked. We talked for a long time. What could we have talked about for so long, so often, we who never talked about ourselves?

We sat down. Later, we stretched out. You took my hand. We continued to talk softly, in almost a whisper that, little by little, died away into silence. Words lost their place, their order, their power. They no longer had value. We stopped talking.

We fell asleep. It is the only time I slept beside you.

Daybreak woke us, daybreak and the noise of trucks passing in the street, making your windows vibrate. You stood up. You turned your back to me. You were so tall. Your shoulders were trembling. I began to be frightened. I held my breath and I pressed my hands very hard to my chest. With your back to me, almost shouting, you asked me to love you. The hoarse and muffled voice you had at that moment, your look of intense anguish when at last you turned toward me because I was quiet, all this I will not forget.

I will never forget you.

But it was too late to invent love. We had become so old, already, with solitude. It was too late. We had the silent gestures, the stifled breathing of love, without anger but with so little desire. . . .

You stayed near me a long time without moving, your eyes closed, your face contracted in a painful grimace. I kept quiet. I felt a tension growing, a spasm in you that reached into my heart.

You opened your eyes. You smiled strangely as if to excuse yourself, just before you began to cry.

You cried. I hurt from your tears, a cruel, sterile hurt that ripped me apart, that bound me to you forever.

You cried. I looked at you. All my fears subsided. I did not touch you. I did not try to comfort you. I fell with you into that otherworld of suffering. I accompanied you. I said nothing.

You cried for a long time. I waited. Slowly you grew calm. I waited some more.

In silence, you showed me the door. In silence, I showed you the bed.

I went out.

The same evening, I was on my way back.

How long the day is in coming . . . how fleeting the night. The sky is clear, without a cloud. There is something absolute in this night, unalterable. I would like it never to end. I would like it already to have ended. One part of me calls for the dawn that another part rejects. I don't know, perhaps I have never known desire to have a single meaning.

The night will end, like pain, submerged in the gray of an uncertain dawn. One knows nothing about the day that will follow.

One day, by means of an innocent remark, he asked why I was following you. The question had astonished you. I waited for the answer. After a while you said, your lips in a smile: No more than I follow her. I remember the bitter look he gave you. He didn't understand. He resented what he believed was your ultimate weakness. On this you never gave in. Yet, it seems to me, one time . . .

No, I'm wrong. A mistake of memory. I was, I had to be, present always. You wanted it. I was there without fail.

The day after we met him, we waited for him in the same café.

All through the last hours of the night we had walked near him. He'd guided us in silence down the narrow streets of what was once a neighborhood. He went ahead of us. He didn't appear to see us. We followed him.

From time to time, at street corners, he would turn. He'd look at you, make a sign with his head, continue. The few people passing by seemed to know him. Now and then, someone would greet him. He wouldn't answer.

The three of us had walked like that until dawn. We didn't know where we were going. I don't think he knew either.

Morning found us at the edge of the river, on the other side of the city. He stopped then and motioned us to sit down on the damp ground. He bent forward to shake your hand, then left without saying a word to you.

The instant, the power of that instant, the instant he left for the first time . . .

I see you. I see us very . . . too well.

He has us sit down. He's going to leave. I feel you shudder near me. He says nothing. You get up. You don't look at me. He walks away into the morning light. He's going to disappear in the meanders of the river. His silhouette shrinks like your eyes that squint with the effort to hold him back yet a while within your gaze. I no longer see him. One can no longer see him. You clutch my shoulders and shake me violently. I'm not frightened, I hurt. I hurt for your clenched jaws, for your lost look that asks for pity. I hurt for your whole body which mistreats mine without knowing it, like someone almost drowned who tries to sink his rescuer in a last spasm of hope. I hurt. I don't draw away. I put my arms around you gently, so gently. I press you against me gently, slowly. I become calm and gentle like the course of a river in summer. I don't want to think. Your head grows heavy on mine. Your rough curls caress my forehead. I must create silence, emptiness, in me to stop the tumult. I hold you in my arms. I mustn't let you go. I cannot give in. I am much stronger than you. You need me so much. I must keep holding you. I hold you.

The sun pierces the clouds. It's cold. I have the feeling you are asleep. I push you away with a delicacy I am unaware I possess. Your eyes are open, fixed on the dull water of the river. You say: We've nothing left but the hope of finding him again. I shiver.

This has to stop. The present is somewhere else, in another place, yesterday, tomorrow perhaps, not now. I don't want these thorns in my flesh today. I don't want it. I cannot defend myself at the moment against this torment.

I shivered. You thought it was from the cold. We went back.

That same evening, we were waiting for him in the café.

Where is the untroubled sadness that induced me to write to you just a while ago? I thought the pain deadened forever, here it comes to life again. The hatred woke it up, hatred and the memory of the deep gash made when he first left you, like a fore-boding. That hatred of him gnaws at me. My mind is scarred by helplessness, by remorse. I did not have the strength. You did not leave me the power to be strong.

For a long time, I hadn't thought about him. I hadn't forgotten him. He was not in my thoughts, as you no longer were. I carried you within me without calling you to mind.

You are within me, forever. You are me. I will never see you again.

For a very long time the pain added to my waiting. I don't want to suffer anymore and wait for you. I don't want to anymore. I cannot anymore.

Already I am weary. The pain is disappearing. The shadows soften. Someone has whispered in me: What good is it?

I am in the center of the night, at the hour when one no longer believes in dawn. A pale moonlight devours the darkness. One could say that it digests the night to prevent the day from ever returning. One could say . . .

One could say nothing. One could say a night of the full moon, banal and solitary. Silence is everywhere. The wind is quiet in the leaves. Time has stopped.

Time stopped after you left. I am ten years older.

You left. A spring followed, a summer, an autumn passed. Afterward, nothing. Now, like yesterday. Ten years.

One night we met him coming across the footbridge that spanned the river. We were on our way back to your place. He had just been there. You slowed down. I sensed you were frightened. I whispered. It's not our fault. You had a strange, tense smile.

He ran toward you. He had a wild look. He caught you and shook you. He was talking. He could not finish his sentences. He was talking and it was incomprehensible. Your name appeared again and again in the middle of a phrase, like a prayer. I had not come near. He seemed ready to burst into tears.

You took him into your arms to calm him. You were looking at me. Over his head, the immense sadness of your look, calling for help. . . . But I could do nothing for you except stay, and I would so have liked to leave, to tear myself away from you, tear you from him. Leave. I stayed.

Later, he let himself be won over. We went back. You held him in your arms. The wind was blowing on the footbridge. It was cold. I walked a few steps behind. Your head was leaning against his, bent over rather, he was much smaller than you. You were talking to him. I heard nothing of what you said. I guessed. I began to suffer, to be afraid. For the first time, I felt totally excluded.

He came to a halt on your doorstep. He was ashen but his eyes were shining. You were already inside. The door was wide open. He, in the middle, between us. I sensed what he was going to say even before he said it. You turned to face him, immobile. You wanted to speak, ask a question. I can't be sure. He thrust a cruel chin toward me. He pointed to me. He asked: Her too? You took your time answering. The silence became sharp, like a knife. You hesitated a long time, a very long time, before answering. I felt you hesitate with every fiber of my body. He was smiling, ironic. He was just about certain of victory. You hesitated. I hurt, hurt badly, from your hesitation. I didn't move. I didn't breathe.

It was almost with an excuse that you let fall: Her too.

He looked me over. We went in.

Why did you hesitate that day? Why did you hurt me so? I was aware of those troubled feelings, that opaque desire binding you to him. I was aware. Why did you make me carry the burden? The three of us were incapable of loving. You knew it well. We could only charm one another, not take risks. We could only hate the defeat, the impotence, in us and cling to our hate, our impotence, like castaways on a raft. You knew it well.

We went in. I was exhausted. I lay down in a corner of the room. I was trembling from fear, from the cold. You brought me a cushion. You covered me with your coat. You poured me a glass of wine. You stroked my face, gently. You left me. You joined him at the other end of the room.

All night long, you talked.

Since you left I no longer see the others. I live alone with some cats, a dog, and silence.

The city is near. I go there only when I have to. No one has ever come here. I visit no one. From time to time, people call me, they have found work for me for a month, sometimes two, never more, I wouldn't accept it. I come back each evening.

Often, in the spring, I take a trip, alone, always. I rarely know where I'm going. Sometimes it is difficult for me to know where I am. I come home before summer begins. The animals are happy to see me. I'm glad to be with them again.

In the village, they know me. They understand that I don't like to talk. At first they asked questions. It was awkward avoiding them. After a few years, they didn't ask anymore.

I'm going to grow old here. My house is the last in the village. Behind it, the forest. Perhaps you would have liked it. It pleases me to think so. It's big. It's empty and bare. I haven't been able to fill it. Winter, when I walk through it, my steps echo on the tiles. Winter only. You know, that resonant quality of the air, in winter, as if it were frozen. Summer, everything is more muted. Autumn and spring, I don't know. It seems to me that these are seasons that linger, that hesitate, waver, uncertain seasons.

I've learned to live with the rhythm of the seasons. In winter, I'm at loose ends. In summer, I walk in the forest. In between, I travel or I wait. I never feel alone. Now and then I take in another cat, I plant a new tree, never in the garden, always in the forest. I like the thought that it owes some of its density to me.

I no longer love anyone now, only trees, animals, and thoughts.

After you left, I tried. Several times, a man opened his bed, his arms, to me. None of the men resembled you. Their eyes lied. They were dry and soft. They never cried.

I'd leave them in the morning, without regret, with a faint tenderness for their inconsistency. On occasion, I would tell them. They didn't understand me. Not one of them tried to see me again.

I stopped from lack of interest.

Where you are, you no longer love anyone. That comforts me. Where you are. . . . But you are in me. I alone watch over you. You need me so.

No one will harm you anymore. No one. As long as I live.

You did not love me. It was impossible for you to love. I did not love you. We felt alive only when we plunged together into the city, into the night. It was our single excuse. Today, each alone, we are no longer anything at all.

Your room was an ark, monstrous but necessary. The ark has foundered. I remain afloat with memories that are waning, and now this furtive revolt rising up the moment I think of us.

You never knew where I lived. We never knew where he lived. We knew we were somewhere in the city, at certain hours of the day. Evening would bring us back to your room.

I always arrived first. You were not expecting me. I think that each evening you were hoping I would come but that it was difficult for you to remember. I never failed you.

I would arrive as the day was falling, when everything turned gray and dull. Whatever the season, I arrived at dusk. I found you as gray as the evening, immobile, your back turned to the window. I'd sit on the edge of the bed. You wouldn't look up at me, but you knew I was there.

Little by little my presence would reassure you. I felt the moment come when you were going to speak. I never understood what you were saying at that hour. You were speaking for yourself alone. I never tried to guess. I waited.

You'd finally get up. I would draw near you. We'd stand for a while at the window, looking at the people hurrying by, the cars with headlights that lit irregularly, then we'd go down to the café.

At times, he'd arrive at that moment. At times, he'd arrive when we were in your room. At times, he did not arrive, he would not be coming.

You would then sink into a mute sadness from which I could just barely stir you. It seemed to you that in his absence nothing had any savor anymore. You had forgotten that there was a time when we knew nothing of him. I accompanied you faithfully during your wandering. We would avoid "his" streets, without mentioning it. We knew, both of us.

Before you left, when he stopped coming back, you were no longer saying anything. You'd utter only a single phrase, just before going out: Let's go. . . . And the night saw us silently cross the city, silently stop in cafés, silently drink and drink some more, silently return to your place. At times I could not bear your silence.

When I could no longer bear to feel you mute, a skeleton, dying from this too great a sickness, I would write to you on the walls, a few words, never a complete sentence. It was a game that we had invented a long time before, well before him, when the night became too heavy and we no longer wanted, no longer were able, to articulate the least sound. We'd write on the walls, one after the other, parallel messages that never ended, as if to leave the door open for a way out.

We would write a long time, until words came back, until the weight of the night eased.

Afterward, I was the only one to write. Never again did you join me. You would look at me as I wrote with eyes that were gentle, absent, asking for pardon. I'd press you to me then. You would let yourself go. I'd stroke your hair for a long time, now and then for hours, until morning.

Only once you grabbed the pencil from my hands, but with such violence. And it was to spell out his name.

The walls of my house are white, were white when I entered it. Now they are beginning to peel. Each day I take note of their slow deterioration. I know that they are like me. It's in the order of things. This order is reassuring. It exists, outside of me. I cannot change it in any way. I don't have to intervene. That's what is reassuring.

My walls are slowly turning yellow. In places they swell up from the pressure of the humidity. My walls are eyes swollen with tears that never burst open.

When it rains, the forest path behind the house erodes. The path becomes a stream all through the rain. One day, perhaps, it will drown the village. The people fear it. Not I. It runs, overtakes me, passes me by to go lower down. It seems to be sending me signals. I think I understand. The forest refuses the rain. It only takes from the storms what it needs to be fertilized. It flings the rest, violence, death, onto the people of the village. I like this new wisdom it has imparted to me. From now on I take from others, those so few others, only what is necessary not to die. The rest I leave to them. That they risk drowning in it no longer concerns me.

There is much to learn, and I have learned much in ten years, about the wisdom of things.

You loved the river. You used to love walking along the river at dawn. Often we would make our way there when the night began to pale.

How sad the river was in the early morning. The glow from the streetlights dulled in its gray water.

We would stop at the foot of the bridges. I used to love, I love, the raging noise of the water that slaps against the pillars. I love this anger of the water which draws back before clearing its way by force down a path, what for me has always been a life-or-death precipitation.

Water, the life of water. This impalpable, fleeting life of liquid stone. This stubborn, absurd will to rejoin the sea, wherever it is, wherever it comes from, fascinating.

We would stay there for a long while, until the sun rose completely, until the hour struck to take you back.

It seems to me that the night grows lighter, that it is losing some of its edge. It's possible that the moon is tricking me again. I don't like it when it is so crude, so arrogant. I don't like nights of the full moon. I know it is going to end. I only need to wait. I wait for the night to dissolve into the mist of dawn. I wait.

I have waited so long since you left.

One evening, long afterward, I went into the city. The night had come very early. It must have been autumn. Rain was falling, quiet rain, penetrating, like thick fog. You know, the terrible rain that rubs out the hours, that lies outside of time, in the eternity of sadness that no longer dares to name itself, autumn rain that erases even the memory of a possible return of summer. It was raining like that. The windows of the stores, lit up, were no longer even a consolation.

I walked a long time, a long time, against the flow of the crowd. I saw the stream of passersby grow thin without altogether taking note of it. I was walking alongside myself, parallel, semiconscious. I walked.

To your place. There was a light at the window. It was impossible for me, then, as now, to admit that someone else was living in your room. I hurried away from the spot, from its attraction. I walked. The impression of escaping from danger persisted. Oncoming cars moved past me. The whistle of the tires on the wet roadway, a continuous whistle, haunting, unbearable, the dull whistle, foreign, that gives a shape of sound to the banality of solitude. . . .

To the station.

I went inside, relieved. I sat down in a corner. I was cold. I was drenched. I waited.

As each train was announced, I'd get up. I would look at the travelers. I was so afraid of missing a face. I wanted to see these men coming from somewhere else. I'd watch the last one disappear, then sit down again until the next train.

I stayed for many hours in that station. At times people approached me, shadows. I saw the fear in their eyes when I said to them: Leave me alone. You are only shadows. They'd leave me alone.

In the middle of the night, someone, a ticket collector, came to ask for whom I was waiting. I said: No one. I had a vague feeling that he was trying to keep me there. I left.

I think it was after that night that I stopped writing you. This evening I begin again, for the last time. This is my last letter.

I am so tired of everything, of this night, of this letter. Memories are of no use.

For a very long time I had not thought about you. Someone else, unknowingly, revived you in me. I can no longer be silent.

I would so like to be older by one night. I would so like to forget you completely, no longer have to fear your presence in me. But you will always be there to eat away my time.

One of the cats has just jumped onto my lap, my beautiful black cat, the oldest, the one that never makes a sound crossing the room. She alone has that disdainful look, that delicate step, that savagery that wells up and then dies down at the moment of a caress as if put on reserve for other battles. She alone has that intelligent silence which reveals the wisdom of a previous life.

She has settled down. She's not startled. I've never done anything that could surprise her.

You remember, in narrow nighttime streets, we'd frequently come upon cats. We tried to curry their favor by meeting up with them again and again. To certain ones, we had given names. They recognized us.

He always stayed in the background. He used to

scorn the childish game that would bind us together as we approached, each time a bit closer, our voices gentle and measured. You would escape from him in this game as in sleep. He didn't like cats. He didn't like you liking cats. They would hiss their hatred about his ankles. I think he was frightened.

He said it, often, he said that I had the eyes of an anxious mother cat defending its little ones. He would put such violence into his words, such aggressive fear, that he made you smile. Still, from a small sidelong glance, from a slight knitting of your eyebrows, I felt your secret gratitude. I know you were thinking of you.

I wasn't able to save you entirely. I wasn't able to defend you from him.

He had the ravenous cruelty of a wild beast. He used to tear, deliberately, with jabs, well placed, repeated. He'd move in a circle, lurking, to prevent any escape. He took pleasure in each stir of revolt, in each avowal of helplessness. You would pay no attention. For a long time he spared you. I knew he wouldn't stop halfway, that a day would come when he would no longer let you escape, even as little as you did then. He used to talk to you about me. You wouldn't answer. You took on an absent expression. Only when I was on the edge of crying out, on the edge of fighting or of collapsing did you ask him to stop. He used to despise you for that, but he would stop.

You did not want to grant me the means to act. You did not want to allow me to defend you to the last. Perhaps you thought that you had grown up. Perhaps you desired him to tear you apart. Perhaps you desired him to put an end to you. Perhaps. Lacking anything else. You desired him so.

I knew you desired him. Always. From the first instant. I wanted to say it to you one night, one night when, once again, he hadn't come.

His visits became infrequent. Sometimes we would remain a week without seeing him. Nothing had yet happened. I believe, I would like to believe, that it was shortly after he had asked you to leave me outside.

That night he hadn't come, we were in your room. More and more often, you refused to go out. We sat near each other, silent. You said my name, in a low voice. I answered. You repeated my name. I understood then that you were calling me. I was near you, but you were calling to me from somewhere far beyond me. I had never felt with such violence that you needed me and that already I could do nothing more for you. You began to moan, almost to beg me, with bits of broken words, unfinished, incomprehensible. You were calling me. I found my name emerging from the lament and I was afraid of recognizing myself.

I held you to me without being able to calm you.

You were crying. It was intolerable. I stroked you gently. For a long time I'd known I was incapable of filling in the grooves your past had dug so deeply. For a long time I'd known that I no longer desired it. I knew that nothing could ever erase the glacial, deadly shadow in you, that it was useless to want to diminish it. I knew. But at the moment you were in pain, I wanted to believe in things possible, I wanted to pull you back. I wanted a way out for you that I knew, also, I could not attain without you. I hoped.

I talked to you about him. I have no idea what I was thinking, but I knew that I must speak to you about him, that it was the only way to have you part with such great suffering. I talked about him.

You stopped crying out, stopped calling. You stopped weeping. You looked at me, an unbearable sadness in your eyes. I averted mine. I hesitated. I hesitated, a little, to say, but I did say. The words scorched my throat. I said them.

You stood up, furious. Your entire body began to tremble with helplessness, despair. You spoke to me as never before. You spoke to me with his shrill, irritating voice, with his words, with such violence, such hatred, of me, of us, that I was not afraid. I knew who was speaking in you. I think at that moment you would have liked to destroy me, not kill me, destroy me, destroy that voice that I embodied but that came from the deepest part of you. You could not hurt me. I was only frightened by the intensity of your desire, by your total incapacity to resolve it, by my total incapacity to help you. I would have liked to give you support. I shared your shipwreck.

I remained still as a rock throughout the crisis. I didn't move, didn't quiver. I knew. I hurt so for you.

Exhausted from rage, you let yourself fall to the floor and you wept, again, for a long while. You seemed to go to sleep. I waited.

I heard that morning was coming by the noise of the trucks as they drove up the street, a more muffled, more dense, less resonant noise, almost continuous. I leaned over you to help you to bed. You weren't sleeping. The eyes you opened to me no longer had that hunted look of other mornings. You looked at me like someone who was starving, who was dying. You said: He'll go away. I won't have the strength to do what I must to prevent it. You put such absolute distress into those words that I understood there was a danger, one day, of your leaving. The desert was there, in you, dry, burning, a desert that was whitening your bones, from the inside, a little more each day. Against this terrifying advance of the desert I could do nothing, only live it with you.

After that night, we never spoke of him again.

I remember now. I knew long before you left that you would leave. I expected you to leave, I didn't fear it. I only tried to put it off. Perhaps I was hoping to hold on to you. Perhaps I was hoping that we would leave together. Perhaps that is what I was waiting for, to have the strength to leave with you. Perhaps. But the morning you left, it seems to me I didn't understand or didn't want to understand. Perhaps you knew that only too well also. Perhaps that is the reason you told me: I'll write you. To cover your tracks, to soothe your conscience, to allow me to keep quiet.

I believed . . . I don't know anymore what I believed. I forced myself to believe that you would come back. I began to wait for you. Even when I knew, I continued to wait for you. You had said to me: I'll write you. You protected me, one last time, from you, from me. Today, I know that with a little luck, a past weighing just a little less, we could have loved each other.

We could have. We weren't able to. You left. I remain here.

Dawn, at last. I could no longer endure this night. I could no longer endure this silence. Dawn came without giving itself away, just when I was beginning to fear my own phantoms. I no longer want to remember. I no longer want to play this cruel, absurd game of an absence that one tries to fill because it hurts too much. To think of you hurts me even more. I don't want it any longer.

Dawn is here, white. Soon the day.
Dawn is here, misty, transitory. I think a bird has

awakened in the forest, a day bird, one of those that is going to leave. Leave . . . but let the birds leave, all of them, let them leave since I'm helpless to hold them back. I could not hold you back. They'll return. You will never return.

Never. Never. Always. How horrible, these words. The moment I think of you, they are there, between us, within me. You chose silence, since you had to choose. You left me words, bloodless words, words sealed up, without hope, without future, petrified words, words set for eternity, words much worse than silence, icy words, prison words, words that keep me nailed, taut, to the floor of your language, words that will find me, with age, intact, physically worn out, but intact. There is no future for me outside of these words which hold so little of it. There is no future for me outside of you. You are in the past. The past is in me. The past, today still, this night, is here. The past is present forevermore. See.

But you cannot see anything, hear anything, understand anything. I would so like to cry out to you my revolt and the horror that comes from us. Your absence forbids it. You cannot hear anything more from me. I have nothing more to say.

Why this unexpected revolt? Why am I suddenly so distraught? For so long a time I have not trembled from emotion like this. For so long a time I've trembled only from the cold. Here I am once again afraid, of you, of me, of this gray and sullied dawn. I'm afraid.

Let me tell you.

My table is near the window. The bed is on the other side of the room, unmade. In the room, disorder. Next to the bed, a pile of clothes that I abandon evening after evening. When the closet is empty, I wash them or I put them away. A kitten sleeps on the quilt, rolled into a ball. He lives. He sleeps. He has much more existence than you, just like the room and the disorder. The things are there, implanted, alive. They protect me from you. They are going to cover the newborn revolt. They will take care of this fresh wound which, a while ago, began to rip my head and chest apart.

I caress the cat seated on my lap. She has glanced at me with mute intelligence. She's not purring. She stays still and looks at me. She has tilted her head.

I would not want to . . . she frightens me. She frightens me all of a sudden. I'm afraid that she's looking at me as I used to look at you. I'm afraid to find myself in her. I'm afraid to resemble you.

It must stop. . . . The circle must be broken. I have already lived too much to let myself be trapped. At this hour, it is necessary for me to have lived too much.

I look out the window. Dawn is asserting itself. The sheets on my bed appear grayer in this pale light. The leaves were hiding their russet hues in the darkness of the night. The birds, more and more numerous, are starting to sing. It seems to me that the city is waking up, though it is too early. I need to believe it. I need its distant hum in the early morning.

The wind has picked up. The earth is brown and

dry on the path. It did not rain the whole night through.

See how this order of things is reassuring. What I was telling you about a while ago.

Already the tempest is calm in me, already I don't understand it anymore. Everything is so simple. Everything is always so simple. See. Even words no longer hurt. They grow weak quickly in contact with things. Things, one no longer names them in solitude, one speaks to them from inside, in a murmur that comes from the soul. One thinks of them without saying anything. They feel it.

The night has been long and full. I am so tired. I'm no longer accustomed to so many words in the silence. They've taken fright. They have infected me with their fear.

In spite of that, through them, I am going to continue to speak. One of us must speak for two.

See how simple life is. To live is so simple. Why do we need so much time to realize it? We could have, together, lived in this house, together, grown old. . . . We could have but we did not know how.

You lacked patience.

Do you know that on occasion I resent you for leaving, for my solitude, for the pain which sneaks up at certain moments and stabs me between the ribs?

We will never leave each other, you used to say. Did you truly believe that I could hold you back? Perhaps. Perhaps he believed it too. Perhaps that's why he detested me so much. Perhaps I hated him because I knew that he alone held the power to prevent me from it. Perhaps.

This accumulation of perhaps between us over the ten years gnaws away at my memory. Sometimes I have the impression that it's rotting. I have trouble finding you among the possibilities.

No. It is still a way of coming upon you in doubt, in uncertainty, in what is unfinished. My memory plays our game of phrases on your green wall. As long as it questions itself, you cannot disappear forever.

Your choosing to play the truant encumbers me each day that passes. This is not a reproach. No more than a cold shadow that weighs on me.

Soon the cats will go to the kitchen to wait for me, begging for food. Soon the city will wake up to the morning's tumult of sounds.

There is something in this sudden daybreak that I don't understand. Your vagueness has faded onto me. It is the first time in a long while that I've let myself be surprised.

Often I fall asleep after day comes. At night, I don't know what I do. I live. Each evening, the dusk is a trial for me. I wait for it to pass seated in an arm-chair, a glass in my hand. It passes.

When night is here, I know that I begin to live. I have not forgotten. I walk in the house. I read.

Almost ten years. So many days. So many nights.

I wanted to live among the fields. I couldn't. Not from fear. No. It would have seemed to me that I was unfaithful to you.

One spring morning I walked along a hallway, I passed through a door, I went out, I looked for the house. That lasted a long time, it seems to me. One day, I came upon it. I saw it. I loved it. It was closed up, for rent.

The house has been mine for almost ten years.

Six o'clock rings at the church. A hazy six o'clock in a jumbled morning. It is already so late. To say to you, to say that I yearned for this dawn with all my body and that it troubles me. I don't understand it. It remains foreign to me. I hear its wind in the forest. I see its chalky mist. I breathe in illusion in its dense humidity, a feeling of illusion, indefinable and men-acing.

The papers pile up on the table, next to me. I didn't know I had so much to say to you.

I must continue.

I remember the last time we saw him. It was raining, that sinister, mean rain familiar only to those who live near a river. He hadn't come. You had stayed silent for a long time waiting for him next to the window. In the middle of the night, I must have forced you to go out. We had gone out. You'd slammed the door of your room in a violent movement of refusal.

We walked a long time. You said nothing. We finally stopped in a café. We drank too much, in silence.

After a while your eyes began to wander. They were less sad. You appeared certain of something that I was unable to perceive. I believed it was the effect of the alcohol. You were drinking more and more, more and more rapidly.

You started to watch the door intently, your eyebrows knit, your forehead lined with concentration. You seemed to have forgotten me completely. It made me dull, dreary. As each man entered, you would recoil toward me, instinctively, with a quick recognition, just as quickly put out.

Little by little I began to understand. I understood. I didn't want to believe that you were waiting for him. For a long time we had stopped talking about him, but I was very much aware of your hopes. You no longer pronounced his name outside of those moments he was present.

He had become aggressive. He did not appear anymore, except rarely, arriving with a loud burst of anger. He had started to hate you. He would come to

measure your capacity to despair over him. He creat-
ed unhappiness. He took joy in it.

You didn't reproach him his absences, didn't
reproach him his cruel words. You hardly spoke to
him anymore. You would look at him, listen to him,
humbly content for the few minutes he granted you.
He would laugh. He would shout and laugh. You,
each time, more dejected. He'd laugh at your dejec-
tion. When he went too far, too low, in his anger, in
his desire to hurt, all you had for him was a look of
painful compassion which would make me tremble
with rage and disgust.

When he came, he no longer stayed until the end
of the night. He would pass by. Shout. Leave again.

In this café, this time, the last, he arrived. I can't
tell how you knew he was coming, if he had let you
know, if it was your intuition. He arrived. I had the
impression that he had been looking for us. He
appeared anxious. He was out of breath, savage. I
saw the fear rise up in you. And the pleasure that this
fear procured. I saw his tension. I realized that we
were about to go under. I shrank back into my chair.
I didn't have the time to fear for myself.

He walked up to you. He started speaking with
that cruel, fluctuating, cutting intonation that in the
past made you smile, which at that moment shattered
you. I knew it. I could do nothing about it. You were
already too deeply lost in fear. I stretched out my
hand to catch hold of your arm. You drew it back, as
if I had burned you. He spoke.

I don't know anymore precisely what he said, but
I felt your body stiffen, your head reduce to nothing
but eyes, your silence become overwhelmed by a

flow of distress. I would so have wanted, so much wanted, to breathe my force into you, put out this fire inside you by my presence. I could do nothing but be quiet, and I kept quiet. He kept talking.

He reproached you for having left your room without waiting for him. He reproached you for his having looked for you. He reproached you for not hoping to see him any longer. His tone became increasingly vehement. With each word his voice turned drier, whiter. He started to reproach you for your inability to live, your constant half measures. He spoke with tight, incisive words that I could not tolerate you hearing.

You had taken refuge in a country where nothing, outside of him, could reach you.

I know that you longed for this cry of love that destroyed. I know it.

He kept talking. He began to gesticulate. He belched out his anger. You remained still, as if absent. He screamed his contempt for you, for your inconsistency. He screamed his bitterness. Were you unaware of that?

In that state beyond himself, he spoke of loving you. He defied you. You became rigid. You squeezed your glass as if to break it, far, far from him, far from me, but so attentive. You said nothing. Why did you wish to go to such lengths to hear him abuse you? It would have been so easy to stop him. I knew the words that one would have had to say. I knew his bitterness, its absolute fury.

You said nothing. You didn't move. You let him talk. He talked. You let him leave. He left. You watched him leave, your eyes wild. You said nothing.

We stayed in that café a long time after he left. I looked at you. You were looking at nothing, inside yourself. Now and then you seemed to discover me with an agonized smile that tore into your eyes.

We continued to drink all night long.

At dawn, you said: Let's leave. It appears to me, at times, that I never again heard the sound of your voice.

That's false and I know it.

So much time passed telling you our story. Absurd time, useless. Fatigue overcomes me. An immense disgust of us both.

I remember too well my cowardliness of that evening, my cowardliness of each evening that followed his departure, all those pallid nights. Waiting for an uncertain dawn. Waiting for your remission to begin.

What was I hoping for? And, above all, what would I have done with you?

He had left and it made me suddenly happy. He had left and I was relieved. For the first time, I betrayed you. I was waiting for the moment when you would recover. I thought you were going to come back to me. I thought you were going to take me, take us, lead us off elsewhere, very far, to a place where memories would never again catch up with us, to a place where little by little we would come to forget ourselves. I betrayed you. I put my hope in his departure as a child hopes in its mother. I believed. I wanted so much to believe. I betrayed you.

After you left, I never, not even once, broke my unspoken word to you. Never again. I owe to it my ten years of silence, my ten years of life half lived.

Why write you this, you who cannot read what I write? Why do I still make use of you?

Dawn is rising in me, inside my head. I must not be afraid. I must not. This night has lasted ten years.

Your lips will never again utter my name. They are filled with earth. What good will it do to make another out of his own absence? What good will it do for me to cling to you again? I can do nothing for you. You were able to say: I'll write you. It is the most terrifying gift one has ever given to anyone.

It is the most beautiful gift.

One night you also said: Other times contain us. We will never be ourselves. We are so many others that live in us just as we possess them.

We are so many others. . . . I will never be any other but you.

I will never be . . . I can say nothing of what will come to pass. Everything escapes me, has escaped me for such a long time. I'm accustomed to seeing the days vanish, the cats grow up, the trees sprout in the forest. I'm accustomed. Yet, each autumn, the same sigh rises in my chest. Each autumn, the same thing that could never become a regret.

Day, the day, is here. I have to see it. Suddenly, everything is jumbled, tangled up. Suddenly, everything is unraveled.

My ten years of silence.

I have passed the age when one can be surprised. I would so like to have passed that age.

I know it now. There is no use in lying anymore. We lived only a winter together, the winter we met, the winter you left. The veil falls away. The curtain rises. Dawn is here, cruel, implacable.

I understand now that it was a dawn like this when you left.

I feel that immense fatigue, somewhat obtuse, that I believe I mentioned a while ago. However, it seems to me it has changed gears, taken a new direction to find me, that it has been transformed because of it, that it contains things possible. It seems to me. I am so tired of trying to know.

I still want to speak to you about you. The holes deepen, grow wider. I am losing the sharp memory of your presence.

One day, where? When? Before, after, his departure? I'm no longer sure of it at all. One day, one night, you wanted to keep me there. You chatted incessantly with a bizarre incoherence, especially evident when you'd try to take a breath, as if the slightest pause would be fatal. You wanted to keep me there. You didn't say it. I stayed, without understanding why, or perhaps I was frightened of understanding you only too well. I stayed, waiting for the moment to leave, waiting for the moment that you would accept my leaving.

I don't know anymore. I have lost the thread. Why did I start relating this to you? What was I trying to accomplish?

You are far, already, very far from me.

I think that I still love you. I think that I have always loved you.

I love you.

An opening has just been made deep within me. Something has torn apart, an image of you or of your silence or of my solitude. Something that concerns both of us.

One day, you will stop hurting me. One day, I will stop caring. I love you. Your absence at this moment is intolerable to me. You had no right. I can no longer bear you. I can no longer bear myself.

We spent so much time walking in the streets, strolling along the river, living only half a life, abandoning the idea of choosing it. So much time. So many winter nights. We talked so much, regretted so much not to be elsewhere, to be other people, to be different. We spoiled everything. We knew it. We were proud of it. We suffered so insanely, so stupidly.

I don't want to be lucid in this new way anymore. I don't want it anymore. I refuse.

I cannot prevent myself from knowing. I cannot prevent your knowing within me. I cannot prevent myself from suddenly understanding. I cannot prevent anything.

You bequeathed me your helplessness. You left me silence and the unformed cry of your rebellion. You left me alone but alive. I will never know if I should thank you for it.

Listen. Morning is here. I would like for you to be able to hear it. I would so like to share it with you.

Your words in my silence for ten years. Morning is here. I didn't recognize it. Yet it is the morning of your last departure. It is the morning when I know well, know too well, that you'll never be able to come back again. It is the morning when I understand, at last, that I must choose.

I would like you not to leave me alone with this

terrible choice. I would like to hold you back one instant more.

Your features blur in my memory. Already I no longer remember the sound of your voice. It was deep. . . . Do not abandon me. You have no right. I held your hand up to the hour of your defeat. Up to the day you left, I held your head in my arms. If you had asked it of me, I would have held your body all through its fall. You asked for nothing.

I don't like this silence of yours now that night is ending.

Help me. Help me. Tomorrow will never be the same again. We must sort out, choose, when time is already consuming us.

Sleep. Give way with fatigue at the edge of this table, the edge of the day. . . . The past escapes me entirely. It was still whole when I held it in my hand a little while ago. It is crumbling. It is dust that returns to my memory from time.

I want to remember once again the vagueness of your look when he said goodbye. I want to remember the silence of our nights after he left, the silence of my years after you left. . . .

Wearing away comes at the hour one expects it the least, the wearing away of memory, lost in the mists of a dawn for which one has stopped hoping. I would like to say more. I no longer can.

You will not be speaking anymore. From now on, I will keep you silent. There are too many of your words on my lips. The ten years have only made them fade. This morning will finally erase them.

You lost your way a long time ago. It's possible that I'm losing my way as well. It's possible that at last

I'm finding myself. This morning, anything is possible.

A new feeling of certainty is rising in me. Masks come undone, one by one, yours as well as mine. I've passed through the hour of pain. It's true that one does not traverse mirrors with impunity. The calm of this dawn is immense. One might say that it is standing still. The calm of the dawn is in me.

Other times contain us, you used to say. At last, today, I am here.

Once again fear has vanished. I know that I do not know how to live. I'm not sure I have the desire. This day will tell me, before night comes. I'm not afraid of knowing. Anything is possible.

It is finished. I will stop writing to you after a few more words.

There is one certainty in me, though I still do not know its secret. It abolishes the time of despair, the time of revolt. It opens the desert door.

Whatever I do now, dawn is here, in me, forever.

About the Author

Marie Bronsard is a novelist, short-story writer, and playwright. She is the author of several books, including *L'Alliance*. Bronsard lives and works in southern France.